The Fairytale Hairdresser

and the

PRINCESS AND THE FROG

Abie Longstaff
&
Lauren Beard

PUFFIN

Kittie Lacey was the best hairdresser in all the land.

It was springtime and the air was full of excitement.
Tomorrow, Prince Freddie would be crowned King!
Fairyland Village was holding a parade to celebrate his coronation.

Everyone was making special floats for the parade.

The Three Little Pigs were building
a float of straw, wood and bricks.

Hansel and Gretel made their float
out of chocolate and sweets.

And Rose, the Sleeping Beauty,
was planning a very soft bed
float covered in cushions.

Prince Freddie was entertaining the crowd with his juggling skills.

"My long-lost cousin Prince Castor has come to stay," he told Kittie, as he threw the balls high in the air. "His moustache needs a trim so I'll tell him to come to see you. Look out for him – he wears a tall hat and has a magic wand."

The next day Kittie's friend Princess Lily came to the salon. Lily was a vet, and she was having a wildlife theme for her float.

"I can't wait to watch Prince Freddie become King!" said Lily. "He's so lovely."
"Freddie is really nice," said Kittie. "I could introduce you to him if you like."
"Oh, Kittie," sighed Lily. "I feel so shy with people. I never know what to say.
I much prefer talking to animals."

Just then a frog hopped into the salon. He seemed very upset.
"Hello," said Lily. She picked up the frog and placed it gently on the counter.

"Look," said Lily. "This frog has a tiny crown on his head."
The frog picked up some clips and began to juggle them.
"That's funny!" laughed Lily.

But Kittie looked at the crown. She looked at the juggling.
"Freddie?" she asked. And the frog nodded.
"What happened?" cried Kittie. "Who turned you into a frog?"

FREDDIE LOOKED AROUND . . .

hmmmm...

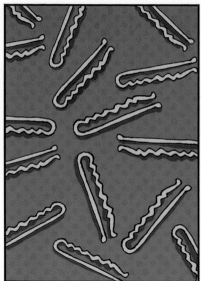

WHAT NEXT . . . ?

?!?

ONE LAST CLUE . . .

A magic wand?

ASKED KITTIE.

A hat?

SAID LILY.

A moustache, a hat, a magic wand... wait... cousin Castor!

SAID KITTIE AND LILY TOGETHER.

Lily gasped. She scooped up Freddie in her palm. "Why would your cousin do something so mean?" Freddie pointed at the crown.

"Because he wants to be King!" Kittie translated. "And if Freddie is a frog, Castor will become King instead!"
Freddie bobbed his head sadly.
"Don't worry, love," said Kittie. "We won't let him get away with this."

They hurried to the castle as quickly as they could.
"Everybody, we need your help!"
cried Kittie as they ran,
and one by one her friends joined them.

But somebody was already
waiting for them . . .

"Stop right there!" shouted Castor.
Kittie spoke up. "You need to turn Freddie back into
a Prince," she said calmly.
"Never!" he replied. "I want to be King!"

"Well, we don't want a King who is mean and cruel,"
said Kittie. "We want Freddie."
"In that case," yelled Castor, "I will turn you ALL into frogs!"
"Quick!" Kittie called. "Everyone, hide!"

But it was too late.

Castor shot a spell at Red Riding Hood and she transformed into a frog!

A spell hit
Mr Gingerbread Man.

Then the
seven fairies.

Soon there were frogs
EVERYWHERE!

What could Kittie do?
She looked at Rapunzel's long plait and it gave her an idea!

First, Kittie pulled a bottle of hair gel from her tool belt and squirted it on the ground . . .

which made Castor slip and slide and tumble to the floor.

Then . . . "Rapunzel, Rapunzel!" Kittie cried. "Let down your hair!"
Rapunzel untied her long plait and
Kittie swung it into the air.

It flicked into a lasso and caught Castor!
He was trapped!

Kittie's friends hopped around her feet.
"How can I turn you back?" she puzzled, picking up Castor's wand.
"I wonder . . ."
She took the scissors from her tool belt
and with a great big

SNAP!

she cut the wand in half.

In an instant everyone was transformed back to normal!
Everyone except Freddie.
"Ha ha ha," cackled Castor. "I put an extra-strong spell on Freddie.
You'll never undo it!"

Tears rolled down Freddie's face.
"It's OK," said Princess Lily. "I'll look after you forever. Even if you are a frog."
She leaned down and gave Freddie a kiss.
There was a flash of light.

And Freddie turned back into a prince!

Freddie laughed – he was
so happy to be a person again.
"Thank you for saving me, Lily," he said.
Lily smiled at him. "Any time!"

"Three cheers for Kittie and Lily!"
cried Red Riding Hood.
And everyone shouted, "Hip, hip hooray!"
"Now let's get on with the parade," said Lily.

Kittie tried
lots of styles
on Freddie to
find the perfect
look for his
coronation . . .

But in the end
only one felt
just right!

Everyone cheered as the floats went by.

"Hooray for King Freddie!" they cried.

But the loudest cheer was for Kittie Lacey,
the best hairdresser in all the land.